The Story of Beowulf

The Story of
Beowulf

Retold from the
Ancient Epic by
STRAFFORD RIGGS
Decorated by
Henry C Pitz

The Junior
Literary Guild

New York · · · · · MCMXXXIV

Foreword

JUST as Conrad's character Singleton, in *The Nigger of the Narcissus*, sat in the fo'c'sle reading, so, on board the Gulf of Akaba, off Cape Verde, I saw Old Man Seastream with a tattered copy of *Beowulf*, which, by some strange chance, had been sent down to the ship as suitable reading for sailors. Off the lonely island of Fernando Naronha, Seastream and I fell into talk just after the third mate had twitted the sailor for reading "them kindergarten fairy tales."

Seastream was in a mood of quiet defensiveness. "There isn't," he said, "much more than a story of how the hero killed Grendel, then Grendel's mother, which was more frightful, then the fiery dragon with only one true man to help. But the tale is a fine one if you get the spirit of it; and it *gets* me. That's what it does—*gets* me."

Strange that I should look back over crowded years to remember that remark. Seastream, unschooled, not only brought me to Beowulf but with his unconsidered words made me see something that should be obvious to all of us, though it is not. It is that what we would see introduced into the life of a nation must be first introduced into the schools, or in other ways carried into the world of youth.

History tells us that the Beowulf epic was forgotten for nigh upon a thousand years and might have been irrevocably lost had not a solitary manuscript been discovered. If some grain of superstition be allowed us, I should hold that among the high gods sits one encharged with the care of literary treasures, so that nothing is utterly lost, but merely forgotten by men because purposely hidden until the proper time arrives when the world is ready to receive, just as the Rosetta Stone, and the tale of Hasisdra, and the monoliths at Tiahuanaca, and the litany scratched on the bricks at Ur were hidden; for had they been found earlier, vandal hands might have marred them. Carrying this belief down to to-day, I like to think that in these days when knighthood is at low ebb, and when the desire for acquisition looms large in the thoughts of men, someone in that workaday hive of New York chanced to hear a whispered word of that guardian god of literature, so bethought himself, or herself, that a tale of heroism, of faith in self, of courage, of patience, of forbearance might find readers in a world too much involved in trivialities. For it certainly seems marvelous to me that this book should appear at this moment, quite as marvelous as that it appeared out of the dark in the nineteenth century when, as now, waves upon waves of broken hopes and desperate efforts dashed against the ship of state, dangerously threatening. For the marvel of that appearance I am grateful as the sailor is grateful for the light. That gratitude is touched with high happiness because the someone who thought to bring a new Beowulf into the world should have found, as illustrator, one whose soul seems "sticht to the starres," whose discernment is rare, who has dared in originality, whose enthusiasm is contagious.

CHARLES J. FINGER

The Story of Beowulf

WHICH TELLS something of the youth and early manhood of Beowulf, how he heard of the monster GRENDEL, and of Daneland.

ONCE upon a time, in the far north of what is now called Europe, there was a kingdom known as Geatsland, and its ruler was named Hygelac. It was a harsh country, with high mountains and narrow stony valleys, and it had a long seacoast with many harbors and inlets, and the men who lived there were famous for their bravery on both sea and land.

Like their neighbors the Danes and the Frisians, the Geats were war-like, and for the greater part of every year Hygelac and his warriors were engaged in fierce battles with various tribes, who would enter the territory of the Geats, to steal cattle and lay waste the fields of grain, and burn the farms of his retainers.

There were other foes, too, to be dealt with. The great caves along the coast were inhabited by all manner of evil monsters that lived partly in the sea and partly upon the land, huge serpents with scales of brass, that patrolled the coast and devoured fishermen when they could be taken by surprise at their nets.

In Geatsland were vast forests where loathsome beasts made their homes in the hollow trunks of dead trees and prowled only by night, feeding upon sleeping pigs and young rabbits and other innocent animals. It was not safe to travel in those woods after dark, and the wandering minstrels who went from place to place in the country-side were careful not to be caught in their ghostly depths.

But for the most part the sea-monsters and the forest terrors kept to their own lairs and seldom invaded the more populous districts. Only when an incautious farmer or fisherman had been foully killed by one of them did the lords of Geatsland wage war upon the strange inhabitants of the coastal caves and the forest fastnesses.

Now, for many years Hygelac ruled over his people with a stern but kind hand. Beside him was his queen, named Hygd, and called the Wise and Fair. About the king and queen were gathered the finest lords of the land. All were valiant warriors whose courage had been tried in many battles. They were tall like the trees of their forests, and broad like the stout

beams of their boats, and each man had the strength of ten. They were yel-low of hair; their eyes were deep-set and burned blue like the sea; on their arms and around their necks were great circlets of beaten gold; and upon their heads they wore helmets decorated with the horns of bulls or the black wings of ravens.

In battle these lords were fierce and terrible, and their war-cries froze the blood of their enemies. But in their own halls, in times of peace, they often dropped their warlike mien and sang and laughed and fondled their dogs and played jokes upon one another like children.

When they gathered in the great drinking-hall of the king, the minstrels would come among them after they had eaten; and with horns of ale passing from hand to hand, these lords of Geatsland would listen to songs of other lands and to news of the world which lay beyond their own frontiers. They heard the stirring story of Sigmund, that great hero; or learned how this king was warring with that or how a terrible dragon had destroyed a whole army of brave fighters.

Sometimes Hygd the Wise and Fair would call upon one or another of the assembled company and beg him to recount some particular deed of valor which he had performed in the past; and often Hygelac conferred with his warriors on some point of warfare or on the building of new boats which would better withstand the fierce gales of the winter seas.

And the younger men listened, their blue eyes wide with eagerness, to the tales of bravery and battle, and struck one another upon the knee, vowing themselves to great deeds when they became older, or boasting of their youthful exploits and feats of strength.

AMONG the number of youths who were in thrall to Hygelac was Beowulf, his nephew. Like so many great heroes of old, Beowulf was the son of his king's sister. As a small boy, Beowulf had shown such strength of body that Hygelac had early named him one of his thanes. So his mother and father gave him up, and young Beowulf went to live with his uncle, to learn the arts of war and the handling of ships.

For several years he led a lonely life, for so great was the strength of his limbs that even among those men of vast vigor he was a youth to be

marveled at. As the years slipped by and he grew to manhood, he became more and more sullen in his strength, and his companions dubbed him "The Silent." His movements were clumsy. He tripped over his sword. He broke whatever he touched. The other youths laughed at him for his awkwardness, but in secret they envied the immense spread of his shoulders and the terrible swiftness of his stride when he hunted in the forests.

When he was sixteen years of age, Beowulf was challenged by one of his companions, Breca by name, to a swimming race in the sea. He accepted the challenge because he had been called lazy, and in his heart he was angry that his strength had never truly been tried.

For five days and five nights he and Breca fought the waves of the sea, until Beowulf reached shore victorious. Later, when he was accused of cowardice in this race, he told the true story of those black nights in the water, and what he related then was to go down in song as a famous legend.

WHEN Beowulf had at last reached the full tide of his manhood, and been admitted to the circle of Hygelac's personal retainers, a feast was held one night in the king's drinking-hall. From all over Geatsland famous warriors and earls gathered at the drinking-benches of their king to hear the songs of the minstrels and take part in games and feats of strength.

The drinking-hall was decorated with the green boughs of fir trees, and fires blazed on the hearths at either end. Along the walls, at intervals, were placed flaming torches which lighted the vast hall with flickering light, and the smoke from the flares and the fires on the hearths was drawn high to the roof, where it disappeared in the gloomy rafters through a hole cut at the peak.

Around the hall stood wooden benches in tiers, one above the other, and at one end, highest of all, was the table at which Hygelac and Hygd his queen sat in their robes of state. The lower benches were crowded with the lords of Geatsland, and waiting upon them with food and drink were their vassals.

In one corner of the hall were piled the armor and helmets of the warriors, and the spears tipped with bright metal, the huge swords glittering in their places. The air was heavy with the smell of burning pine and fir. There was not much laughter among the guests, for these were men of the North, noted for their silence. But now and again a clear deep voice rang out above the continual murmur of the crowd and there was an answering rise in the applause or disapproval of those who heard.

Beowulf   Here and there stood a huge dog, resting his head upon his master's knee and waiting patiently for a rough caress or a chunk of meat. The servants hurried from bench to bench with ox horns adorned with beaten gold and filled with heady mead, that favorite drink of the Northmen, flavored with honey. Large wooden bowls painted in bright colors and overflowing with various meats stood on the tables and were dipped into by the seated guests.

Hygelac and his lady were served separately, from dishes more beautiful and precious than the rest, and the queen paused often to acknowledge with her gracious smile the toasts of her subjects as the drinking-horns were raised and held toward her. The king ate and drank sparingly, as became an old man, but the queen (who was almost young enough to be his daughter) took a lively interest in everything that was placed before her.

At the feet of the royal couple sat Beowulf, at a table especially prepared for the king's earls. These were the most favored and beloved of all the warriors of Geatsland. But many were the murmurs of jealousy and discontent among the lords when they beheld young Beowulf in such a place of honor.

"Who," they asked among themselves, "is this sluggard Beowulf, that he should sit directly below our king?" And some answered, "It is because he is the son of our king's sister and brave Ecgtheow; and because he has the strength in his arms and legs of thirty men."

The older lords shook their gray heads disapprovingly and the younger men sighed and scowled with jealousy. Only one spoke up in defense of Beowulf, an ancient warrior with white flowing locks and a gentle sweet voice.

"Look you, you foolish ones," he said. "It is written in the stars that this Beowulf whom you call sluggard will one day be famous in song and story for his deeds of surpassing bravery and strength."

But when the others questioned him further, the old man smiled a wise smile, and would say no more; and as he was considered something of a sage and a magician, they exchanged wondering glances among themselves and kept their tongues quiet.

But Beowulf, unmindful of the talk about him, sat in gloomy silence. He ate little, but each time the drinking-horns were passed he drank long and deep. And like his drafts of ale and of mead, his thoughts, too, were deep and long.

His strength was great, but there was no use for him to put it to, and he longed for wild adventure and the chance to stretch his muscles to the limit of their power.

True, he thought, I have fought small dragons and hunted wild boars, but such hazards are mere games for boys, and I am now a man. My uncle Hygelac is at peace with his neighbors, and there is no war in which I can take part. He sat stonily in his place, and his blue eyes were scornful of the earls about him and their big talk of little battles.

Then, at a signal from Hygelac, the murmur of voices died down, until there was no sound in the whole length of the vast hall save the spluttering of the flares upon the walls and the snarling of two dogs over a chunk of meat on the earthen floor.

"My brothers," spoke the king, "there is among us this night one who has come a long way over the sea and the land. He brings, he says, a wondrous song for you to hear. It is long since we have had word from the North, and this man's harp is a sweet one. Sing to us, Wanderer, that we may have your news and your entertainment."

Then the minstrel came forward with his harp. He was a tall rugged man, with a beard streaked with gray. He had the air of one who had traveled long distances, and his blue eyes were wide and fixed like one used to watching the horizon of the wide world.

Around him was wrapped a cloak of deep blue, held together by a curious clasp of gold. Beowulf, noting the clasp, thought it resembled a coiled snake, for there were two green stones set in it which glittered. This man, Beowulf thought, has been in far-away places. He will chant us a good song.

Then the Wanderer (for so he was called) sat down upon a wooden stool, threw back the cloak from about his arms, and with long thin fingers struck the resounding strings of his harp.

He sang in a sharp voice that was like the crying of birds on the gray sea, but there was a sweetness in it at the same time which held his hearers,

and the lords of Geatsland leaned forward on their benches in eagerness to catch every word.

He sang of the vast and frozen North, where winter lay upon the land for many, many months, and men fought in the gloomy light of the night-burning sun.

He sang of endless forests stretching black and forbidding in a sea of snow; of mountains higher and bleaker than the highest mountains of Geatsland; of the strange and fearful demons that inhabited this ghostly region.

He sang of dragons that had no blood in them, but which, when they fought in bitter combat among themselves, oozed a white liquid so cold that even the fir trees withered where it fell.

He sang of the limitless gray sea and the green-white icebergs floating treacherously, and of the sirens who lived in caves upon them, and whose bodies were clothed in blue fish scales and whose hair was swaying seaweed.

He sang of the monsters of the deep, strange wormlike creatures with brazen heads and tails like the tails of serpents, and Beowulf nodded with a knowing air, because he had swum in a great race against Breca and had learned something of the sea and what it held of terror for the swimmer.

Then the tune of the Wanderer changed. His voice fell to a lower note, and he sang of Hrothgar who was king of the Danes, that country not far from Geatsland, across the water.

He told a sad story of desolation and despair in Hrothgar's land, because of a beast which had struck mortal fear into the hearts of the lords of Daneland. For on one cruel night, twelve years before, there had come to Heorot—which was the great drinking-hall of Hrothgar—a monster, part animal, part man, part bird. The lords of Daneland were sleeping soundly in Heorot, and the monster, who was called Grendel, had forced open the solid doors of the king's hall and carried away in their sleep thirty of the greatest earls of the Danes.

There had been lamentation throughout the land, and many were the attempts to slay Grendel, but none had succeeded. And Hrothgar and his councilors no longer dared to sleep in Heorot, since for twelve long years Grendel repeatedly visited the king's hall and wrought destruction there. Yet Heorot had been well built by Hrothgar and for twelve years it had withstood the monster's onslaught, but in those twelve long years the valiant young warriors of the king had not withstood so well the nightly visitations, and now the land was despoiled of its youthful strength, and there remained to the king only those fighters whose early vigor had long since passed, and Daneland had become a country of old men and defenseless women.

The Wanderer sang of the fear that was in the Heart of Hrothgar the king and in the hearts of all his vassals and retainers, of the sorrowing of the women who were the wives or mothers or sisters of the slain warriors.

He told of Unferth, who was Hrothgar's beloved companion, and how Unferth had not once offered to meet Grendel in combat, because the fear in his breast was greater than his love for his master. And at this a scornful murmur ran through the company that listened, and the lords of Geatsland condemned Unferth for a black coward.

Now, all the while that the Wanderer was singing, Beowulf sat as one bewitched. Those about him paid no heed to his rapid breathing, and failed to notice the light that had sprung into his blue eyes.

He leaned forward upon the table, his arms folded under his still beardless chin, his eyes fixed upon the minstrel. Now and again he lifted his head and shook out the fair hair that hung beneath the golden band encircling his wide white forehead. The huge bracelets that weighted his wrists gleamed like his eyes, and the jeweled collar about his throat was tight because of the swelling veins of his neck. The thoughts that ran through his head were confused, but one idea held sway over all others:

He would seek out this monster Grendel and slay him—yes! slay him with bare hands, these very hands that gripped each other now upon the table until they showed white beneath the pressure of the fingers. His muscles under the armlets of beaten gold rippled like water ruffled by a breeze. He saw himself face to face with the monster Grendel, and suddenly a wild cry broke from his lips and he leaped from his seat.

"Lords of Geatsland and earls of Hygelac," he shouted, as the minstrel finished the song, "I am the son of Ecgtheow and of Hygelac's sister, and in olden times this Hrothgar was a war-brother of my father. Therefore I claim kinship to him, and I will go to the land of the Danes and serve their king. I will slay this Grendel!"

Then among the lords of Geatsland there rose a murmur of wonder at Beowulf's daring, but their wonder was touched with mockery that the Sluggard should dream of combat with such a fiend as Grendel. And they

knew not whether to laugh or to shout with approval when they saw this youth, who had but lately come to manhood, standing before them, his eyes flashing fire, both hands up-flung.

There was great confusion in the hall of Hygelac, and the earls called to one another, and dogs barked. But Hygd the queen stood up amid the turmoil, and holding a jeweled cup in her two hands because of its weight, stepped down to where Beowulf was, and offered him the cup, and smiled at him in affection and pride.

Once again Hygelac commanded silence among the guests in the drinking-hall, and turning to Beowulf said in a loud voice:

"The time has come, O Beowulf, for you to prove your worth. The gods have gifted you with the strength of thirty men, and this strength you should use to the advantage of your fellows. Our neighbor Hrothgar is in sore need. Go forth, then, from Geatsland to the land of the Danes, and do mortal combat with this Grendel-fiend to the glory of Geatsland and the satisfaction of your new manhood.

"But I charge you, Beowulf, son of Ecgtheow, earl of the Geats, and my own nephew, return not to these halls if you should fail in your attempt. Again I say to you, you have great strength. Go you, Beowulf, and use it nobly!"

Thus spoke Hygelac the king, and great was the shout of approval that went up from all the lords of Geatsland as they crowded round the brave young Beowulf. For here was a Beowulf they had never known before, and they greeted him for the first time as one of themselves, and not as a sullen boy whose strength had been so great that he had been made to seem a fool for it.

Then Beowulf drank from the jeweled goblet of Hygd, called the Wise and Fair, and he fell on his knees before his uncle Hygelac and received the king's embrace.

FOR seven days and seven nights there were great preparations in the halls of Hygelac the Geat, that Beowulf might go on his adventure fully equipped for whatever awaited him in Daneland. From the group of companions who had come to manhood at the same time as himself, Beowulf selected fourteen earls to accompany him. He had wished to go alone to the land of the Danes, but his uncle the king had commanded that he be suitably companioned on such a voyage, so that at the court of Hrothgar it could not be said that Hygelac had sent the youth upon a fool's errand and badly equipped. So, with the best grace he could muster (for Beowulf was stubborn, as you have seen and shall see again) he named his earls, and Hygelac ordered that they be furnished with the finest head-pieces and spears and swords in the kingdom.

Special shields were made, of stout wood covered with thick hides and bound with iron and studded with golden nails. Rich cloaks of scarlet and blue there were for the warriors, and massive bracelets of fine gold for their arms and wrists, and collars of gold wire for their throats.

When at last they stood ready in the mead-hall of Hygelac, they were a fine company of young men, whose like was not to be seen in all the countries of the North. Each stood well over six feet in height, with broad shoulders and sturdy legs; and each was as swift of foot as a reindeer.

But Beowulf overtopped them all in stature and in strength and in the speed of his running, and as Hygd beheld him she thought: This is indeed a fine son that my husband's sister was mother to, and his father Ecgtheow would have been a proud man to look upon him.

Hygelac made a speech to the fourteen earls and charged them to be faithful to Beowulf and to the tradition of the Geats in battle. He put them

under the command of Beowulf, and urged them to obey their lord in every particular and to find no service too difficult to render him and no hardship too great to endure for his sake.

Then he turned to Beowulf, and gave the earls into the young man's keeping and begged him to uphold the honor of Geatsland and of his king. Then he nodded to Hygd, who stood beside him clad in a marvelous soft robe of red, her lovely arms covered with bracelets of green gems, and took from her hands a golden collar which he clasped about the throat of his nephew. As Beowulf knelt to receive the gift, a great shout went up from the assembled company, swords were brandished in the air, and there was a tumult of excitement in the high hall of Hygelac.

Then came the signal for the journey down to the beach where a ship lay in readiness to receive Beowulf and his earls, and with torches flaming in the grayness of approaching dawn, the company took its departure.

THE way led for a little time through woodland cleared of all underbrush, where at night and in the light of the flares the company seemed to be passing through some vast mysterious dwelling-place; so tall were the trees that their tops could not be seen and the tree trunks looked like the mighty pillars of a huge hall.

As they passed, the birds that slept in the branches of the trees wakened because of the light, and thought it must be daytime, and flew about calling to one another that the dawn had come. And the little animals scurried underfoot, not knowing what to make of this strange disturbance, and squeaking or growling to warn their small comrades.

At last the hall-like forest gave way to a wide open meadow, and the breath of the sea, damp and salt-smelling, struck the nostrils of the marching warriors. And finally they heard the waves breaking against the headlands not far away, and the moaning of the wind among the rocks of the coast.

As the first streaks of dawn began to touch the dim sky, the company reached the shore.

There, ghostly in the half-light, hung their ship, its prow nosing into the sandy beach, its body rising and falling with the gentle waves of the landlocked cove. Then, as the sun began to touch the towering mountains that hemmed them in, the torches were one by one extinguished.

The wind died suddenly, as it does at sunrise, and the wide sails of the ship hung motionless in the calm. But when the sun at last rose and flooded the world with its warm light, a fresh breeze sprang up.

Beowulf called to the company to hasten aboard, and with much shouting and waving of arms and shields, the fourteen earls clambered into the ship. The vessel was loosed from her moorings; her painted oars were dipped into the water, her sails bellied with the young wind, and slowly she found her way down the harbor to the open sea.

For many hours the sturdy ship fought the waves that crashed and thundered against her sides. For many hours Beowulf and his fourteen companions saw the marvels and terrors of the wide sea.

All kinds of strange monsters, both large and small, were seen on that voyage—playful fishes with scales as blue as the sky overhead and bright small eyes, and long sea-serpents which followed the wake of the ship for hours, turning and rolling in the sea, and looking so evil that even the brave warriors shuddered at the thought of falling into their slimy coils. There were sea-lions of shaggy mane, and bird-like fish with horny claws.

But they came at length to the coast of Daneland and the sea boiled white between them and the land, and the land itself was scarred and pitted with a thousand narrow inlets, which were treacherous to seafarers unfamiliar with them. The forests that clung to the shore line were half hidden in gray mists that moved and twisted like smoke about the trees.

Then, as the adventurers thought they had at last found the entrance to a safe harbor, a mighty storm arose. The land was blotted out with menacing clouds, the waves beat upon the ship with fury, the wind howled through the rigging, and fear darkened the stoutest hearts.

For a time Beowulf's earls tried to prevail upon him to turn away from that black coast, saying that they would be dashed to pieces on the rocks, but Beowulf turned a deaf ear and urged his captain forward.

Then, as by a miracle, they found entrance to a narrow inlet, and the sudden protection of the land stilled the fear in the warriors' hearts. Their sails tattered by the wind, they plied their oars with a great good-will, and as the storm lessened, they beached their boat on a tiny strip of sand at the edge of a deep forest hung with gray fog and silent as death.

No sooner had they landed, however, than they were accosted by an old man, hoary with years but fearless of eye and with a mighty hand ready upon the long spear that stood by his side. Addressing himself at once to Beowulf, he asked:

"Who are you, stranger in Daneland, that you beach your boat with so much confidence upon these shores?"

And Beowulf answered, standing tall in front of his earls:

"I am Beowulf, and I come from my uncle, Hygelac, the Geatish king, and I am a friend to the Danes."

· 24 ·

"That is good," replied the Guardian of the Beach. "I can see by your height and breadth and strength that you are a leader of these fine men who stand behind you. The name of your king is not unknown to me, his fame has long since come to these parts. You and your men are well armed, but I can see by your faces that you come to this unhappy land with no bad intentions. Tell me, Beowulf, what is your errand? For you must know that this is a dead country, that has been dead these twelve years past, that our hearts have no joy in them, and that Hrothgar, our king, is bowed by sorrow in his age."

"I know that well, Guardian of the Beach," Beowulf replied, "and it is to help your good king that I and my earls have come to Daneland."

"Welcome, then, O Beowulf, to these sad shores," the Guardian cried. "Our king will better receive you than it is in my poor power to do. Leave your ship in my care. I will see that no harm comes to it. But I dread beholding such a fine company of young men coming on this fell business. For the fiend Grendel, who has robbed Hrothgar of his rightful estate, and destroyed so many proud young warriors of our kingdom, is terrible beyond words to describe."

But Beowulf cut his discourse short, and begged the Guardian of the Beach to direct them to the hall of Hrothgar, that they might make themselves known to the king, and rest themselves after their long, tiring day at sea.

Then the old man took them a little way into the forest, and pointed out a path to follow, and bade them farewell. And Beowulf and his earls set out at last upon their great adventure in the land of the Danes.

WHICH TELLS of Beowulf's reception among the Danes, his encounter with GRENDEL and with GRENDEL'S MOTHER.

ON AND ON, through the vast, dense forests of Daneland, Beowulf and his companions toiled, until the sweat stood out in drops upon their faces, and their strong legs ached with the weariness of tramping. Their way led through dense underbrush and deep thicket, and Beowulf thought that it must have been many a long day since this passage to the sea had been used.

Finally the path straightened out, and they entered a long vale which suddenly broadened into a marshy meadow, dank and evil-smelling from the vapor which curled from its soggy earth. At the end of this swampy place stood the vast hall of Heorot, the greatest mead-hall in all the wide Northland. About it were clustered the abodes of Hrothgar and his retainers, and scattered here and there, desolate and forsaken, were the farms and dairies of the ill-fated king.

Over all this sad scene there was the odor of death and decay. The fields were untilled, the houses falling down for want of repair, and no human being was to be seen anywhere. Beowulf and his men entered a lane, and the clanking of their armor and their swords was the only sound to be heard as they picked their way along the weed-grown path toward Heorot.

They came to the hall gates, which stood ajar and swinging loosely on their hinges. For twelve long years the plague of Grendel had haunted the vast hall till it became a place of death instead of feasts and rejoicing.

Thrice Beowulf knocked upon the gates, until the king's Herald appeared and asked in a frightened voice whence they came and what they wanted. Beowulf ordered the man to inform his master the king that warriors from Geatsland were come to visit him, and craved food and a place to sleep. The man hurried away, with many a backward glance of fear at the proud array of these fifteen noble visitors in their shining armor.

While they waited for the king, the men from Geatsland looked curiously about them, and peered into the dismal hall which in other days had been so famed throughout the countries of the North. Its once shining gold-bright pillars were now cobwebbed with the years. The benches were moss-grown. No fine hangings were upon the walls. And on the hearths no fires were blazing.

Then presently there was the sound of footsteps, the clanking of armor, and Beowulf and his earls stood ready to greet Hrothgar the king.

First came a company of elderly warriors (for Grendel had killed and eaten all the young heroes of the court). Then the king himself appeared, wrapped in a rich mantle. He was an old man, with flowing white beard, strong hands, and eyes that told their own story of sleepless nights and harassed days. As the party approached Beowulf, the king, with hands outstretched, advanced with firm steps toward the Geatish lords.

"I bid you welcome, O Strangers," was his greeting, "for I can see at once that you come upon a friendly errand into this unhappy kingdom. Tell me, I pray, whence you have journeyed, for my trusty Herald tells me that you ordered him to me, and would say nothing of yourself or of your business. Speak, my friends, for it is not proper that I should remain in igno- *Beowulf* rance of your identity."

Then Beowulf answered in a loud voice, "I am Beowulf, Prince of Weders, son of Ecgtheow and nephew to that good man Hygelac, King of Geatsland. These my fellows have joined me in coming to the land of the Danes, that we may deliver you from this arch-fiend Grendel of whom we have heard dread things."

"Beowulf, son of Ecgtheow!" cried Hrothgar. "Why! this is in truth the son of my old war-brother, my friend! For Ecgtheow and I were comrades in arms many years ago, before sorrow came to Daneland. I knew you, Beowulf, when as a child you played about your father's hearth, pulling the ears of his dogs so that they cried out in pain and astonishment that one so young could have such strength in him.

"Welcome, son of my old friend! You are very welcome in Daneland, and from this day Heorot shall be yours. But I warn you, it is to Heorot that Grendel comes so frequently, greedy for youths to devour, and it is in Heorot that you will meet the demon.

"But come, let your earls lay down their weapons, and remove their armor, and seek rest. There will be feasting to-night in Heorot, and Wealhtheow, my queen, will pass the drinking-horn among you in token of our friendship for you and your brave companions."

Thus speaking, Hrothgar turned to his attendants and bade them prepare the hall for Beowulf and his warriors, and there was preparation everywhere for the feast that was to be held for these visitors from far-off Geatsland.

THAT night, after Beowulf and his companions had rested, for the first time in twelve years there was a great banquet in the hall of Heorot. The place was decorated with fine hangings, the gold-bright roof burnished until it shone like the sun, and the benches scraped and polished by many willing hands. Huge fires were built on the hearths, and the smell of roasting meats pervaded the hall.

Then the company assembled to partake of the meat and wine of Hrothgar, although the ranks of the king's earls had been sadly diminished through the evil deeds of Grendel. In all, it was not a very joyful gath-

ering that night in Heorot, and the twelve-year dread of Grendel lurked in the hearts of the Danes.

In the king's high place sat Hrothgar, arrayed in a fine red robe of lamb's-wool, a golden crown upon his white locks. Beside him was his queen, Wealhtheow the Beautiful, dressed in garments of snowy whiteness, embroidered with bands of silver, a silver circlet on her fair brow, silver

· 33 ·

bracelets on her slim wrists. Her hair was the color of bright copper, and she wore it in two straight braids which fell on either side her face.

The tables were spread with viands such as warriors crave and there was much mead in great cups. The drinking-horns were passed from hand to hand, and many healths were drunk that evening to Beowulf and his earls, and many cups were raised to the destruction of Grendel.

Beowulf sat in the place of honor at Hrothgar's feet. He was clothed in scarlet and gold, with gold bracelets upon his mighty arms, a golden wire necklet of his king's giving about his throat.

To his right sat Aescher, the close companion and trusted counselor of Hrothgar. He wore a blue mantle over his broad shoulders and costly jewels glinted on his breast.

On Beowulf's left was Unferth, the king's favorite, of whom the Wanderer had sung in no uncertain terms concerning his lack of bravery. He was lean and black of hair, with a black divided beard, and he was dressed from head to foot in black and silver.

Aescher leaned toward Beowulf and engaged him in deep converse, enjoying his company, and praising him for his valor. But Unferth, the black son of Ecglaf, sat moody in his place, scarcely touching the meats before him, and drinking only lightly of the mead as it was passed to him.

A gloom hung over the vast hall, and only the noble lords of Geatsland were gay in that sad company. They talked a great deal, and praised everything about them, especially the hall of Heorot with its gold-bright roof, a hall larger and more magnificent than anything they had ever seen before.

Then they fell to boasting of their leader Beowulf, and spoke pridefully of his strength and virtue. In this they were upheld by Aescher, who had heard of Beowulf's feats of strength. And while they talked and toasted one another in the bright ale, Unferth the Black lapsed more and more into sullen silence, and offered no word of praise to Beowulf, and never once lifted his beaker to the lord of Geatsland.

Beowulf noticed this presently, and turning to Unferth said, "You are very silent, O valiant son of Ecglaf. Come, let us hear your deeds of valor, that we may in turn praise you. Speak, friend Unferth, that I may drink from your cup with you."

Then Unferth, the son of Ecglaf, rose in his place, and his look was blacker than the night which hung over the land of the Danes. The torches flaming against the walls flickered on his cheeks, which were paler than the cheeks of a dead man.

"Beowulf!" he cried, and there was scornful anger in his tones, "Beowulf! Look you, my noble earls of Daneland, at this stripling who comes so proudly among us, saying that he will deliver us from Grendel's toils and spells!

"Who is this boy, beardless and white of skin, that he should come over the sea-fields in a boat with his fourteen thanes? Where are his vaunted courage and strength, I ask?

"For let me tell you: Once upon a time this same Beowulf swam a race with one Breca, another young lord of the Geats, called the Bronding, and the story of that race is a shameful thing for honest men to hear. For in this race with Breca the Bronding, Beowulf failed almost before he had started, and the Bronding beat him sorely, so that my lord Beowulf was the laughing-stock of his uncle's court, and ever since he was a boy he has been known for his sluggard nature and his avoidance of battle and his sloth in hunting.

"And I say to you, my brothers, put no trust in this pale upstart. What the Danes have been unable to accomplish, this stripling from Geatsland

HENRY C. PITZ.

cannot hope to achieve. Let him, I say, go back to his own country and swim honest races with his fellows, and not remain here to mock those in

sorrow."

And Unferth folded his hairy arms over his silver breastplate and glared at Beowulf in rage and hatred. For it must be remembered that this same Unferth, the son of Ecglaf, had never undertaken to fight for Hrothgar the king, against the fiend Grendel, and he was wroth with all those who had done so in his stead. Many words of advice had he offered, to be sure, concerning this attack, but never once the strength of his black arms.

Now Beowulf rose in anger, also, and faced the dark brooding Unferth, but he had his anger and his tongue in better control than his adversary, because he knew the words spoken against him to be false, and he replied softly, but in a clear voice, to the accusations against him.

"It is true," he began, "that I was called Sluggard when I was a boy, but I have killed my dragons with the best of my companions, and no one has ever called me coward. What have *you* done, O Black Unferth, against the arch-demon Grendel?"

Unferth made no answer, and sulked shamefully in his seat, his face averted from the gleaming Beowulf who stood so tall above him.

"And as for Breca," Beowulf went on, "that man and I swam a great race, and all know that during it I battled against vast odds, and came out victor. We plunged into the sea, the Bronding and I, and we were in full battle array, and carried swords in our hands to ward off the dangers of the deep. And for five days and nights we fought the sea-demons and the winds and the waves. Until finally I was cast ashore in some place far from home and I was forced to make my way back on foot, and alone. All Geatsland can swear to my valor, O son of Ecglaf, and no one until to-night has ever dared call me coward. I charge you, Unferth, to take back those foul words.

It is not honorable that I should come to Daneland with my lords, in all friendliness offering to render service to your country and to your king, and be called a coward!"

From both Danes and Geats a murmur of approval went up for these noble words, and Hrothgar the king stood up in his place and spoke for the discomfited Unferth.

"All have heard," he said, "the temperate words of Beowulf, and they are the words of a hero. Beowulf will, I know, forgive us if one among us has spoken unwisely, for in our hearts there has been sorrow these twelve long years, and sorrow long continued oft wears down the spirit and makes the tongue bitter with reproaches that we do not truly feel.

"Come now, my queen," he said to Wealhtheow, "pass the great cup among the lords of Geatsland, and give Beowulf first to drink. This is no time for foolish quarrels, and I enjoin you all to be of one mind and grateful to these young and noble men who have braved the wind and the waves to come to us in a time of need."

With these words, Hrothgar lifted to his lips the jeweled cup that Wealhtheow brought him, and then his lady took it again from his hands, and went down from the king's high table and came near to Beowulf.

He took the cup from her and drank deep from its golden depths, and then Wealhtheow went from one to another of the Geatish earls, and each drank in his turn to the glory of Hrothgar and his queen, and to the destruction of Grendel.

After this exchange, the banqueting was resumed with a good will, and many were the speeches made by the Danes praising the land of the Geats, and the earls of Hygelac were loud in their praise of the noble and venerable Hrothgar and his lady, Wealhtheow the Beautiful.

Then the king rose and gave the signal for their withdrawal. Taking his queen by the hand, to lead her from the hall, he turned to his retainers and said:

"It is time, now, that we hasten to our bowers. Come, my friends, let us away from here, that Beowulf and his earls may rest after their travel. And the gods grant that Grendel come not this night to trouble their sleep."

Then summoning Aescher and Unferth to his side, and with his hand upon his queen's wrist, Hrothgar departed from Heorot and left Beowulf and his companions to whatever fate might await them in the darkness of the deep night.

HE fires were burnt out on the hearths when the last of Hrothgar's train had departed. Then Beowulf and his companions set themselves to fastening tightly the door of the hall. They secured it with wooden bolts and tied it with leathern thongs, and so strong was it that no mortal could have passed through.

Then the warriors of Geatsland unfolded their cloaks upon the benches and laid themselves down to slumber, and Beowulf stretched his great length upon the dais of the king, and resolved that through the long night he would never once close his eyes. Near the door lay the young Hondscio, Beowulf's favorite earl, who swore that if any one broke through the door of Heorot he would be the first to give the intruder battle.

Silence crept over the shrouded forms where they lay upon the floor and benches, and there was no sound save their steady breathing and the faint sighing of the night-wind in the trees about the hall.

Beowulf, upon his couch, lay still as death, but his eyes moved here and there in the deepening gloom of the hall, and his breast rose and fell evenly with his breathing.

Outside, a fog was creeping up from the sea, obscuring the moon in milky eclipse, and at last there was not even the sound of the wind in the trees. To Beowulf the deep silence seemed full of moving things invisible to human eyes.

Gradually there came over him a kind of drowsiness that he fought to ward off. His eyelids fluttered against his eyes, and then he swooned with a sleep that lay upon his weary limbs like a heavy garment.

And the fog thickened and wound itself about the vast mead-hall in thick veils of damp gloom. The moon faded in the fog's depth, and the trees dripped with moisture, and the sound of this dripping was the only sound that came through the night.

But suddenly there was a rustling among the wet trees, and a noise like the deep grunt of a pig, but soft and low, startled the fog-bound night, and the drops of mist-water on the trees fell sharply to the ground like heavy rain. Then the fog parted evenly, and in the wide path it made through the night a Shadow loomed gigantic in all that was left of moon-light.

Slowly, slowly it neared the great hall of Heorot, and the night shuddered at its coming, and behind it, as it moved, the fog closed again with a sucking sound. And the Shadow stood before the great door of the hall, and swayed hideously in the ghastly light.

Within Heorot there was a deep stillness, and Beowulf and the Geatish earls slept soundly, with no knowledge of what stood so evilly beyond the door. For the monstrous Shadow was the fiend Grendel, and standing there in the fog-strewn night he placed a spell upon those who slept in Heorot, and the spell he wove was a spell to make sleep more soundly those who already slept.

But Beowulf hung between sleeping and waking, and while the spell did not completely deaden his senses, it so ensnared his waking dream that he fought desperately against it in his half-sleep and was not quite over-powered. This Grendel did not know as he placed his great shoulder to the door of Heorot, while Beowulf on his couch tossed in the nightmare that possessed him.

Little by little the thongs that secured the door gave way, and the huge wooden bolts yielded under the pressure that was strained against them, but no sound broke upon the silent struggle that went on between Grendel and the door.

Beowulf tossed and turned in waking, but the other earls of Geatsland fell deeper and deeper into the swooning sleep.

Then with a rush, the door flew wide, and the fog and salt-smelling night swept in and filled Heorot with strange odors. And in the doorway, swaying this way and that, stood Grendel, huge and dark against the dark night, the fog weaving about him in white veils, and the door of the hall limp on its hinges.

And Beowulf came out of his dream-spell and saw what stood so vast and evil in the doorway. But his eyes were heavy with the spell that clung to him as the wisps of fog clung about the body of Grendel, and only slowly was he able to distinguish the monster. Through his nightmare, now, there came the sense of what had befallen him, and he strove to cast the last remnant of the magic from him as he saw the great form of Grendel swoop down upon the innocent form of young Hondscio, catch him up in enormous hands, and tear him limb from sleeping limb.

And Beowulf struggled, and on the earthen floor of Heorot Grendel swayed with his prey.

And now at last Beowulf saw what manner of thing this Grendel was. His legs were like the trunks of trees and they were covered with a kind of gray dry scale that made a noise like paper as the fiend moved this way and that. The body of the beast was shaped like that of a man, but such a man as no mortal eyes had ever before beheld, and the size and shape of it were something to be marveled at.

The head was the head neither of beast or man, yet had something of the features of both, and the great jaw was filled with blunt fangs that ground the bones of the unhappy Hondscio to pulp. Shaggy matted hair hung over the low forehead, and the eyes in the face of Grendel were the color of milk.

Horror-struck upon his couch, Beowulf felt his limbs in thrall and could move neither leg nor arm to raise himself as Grendel devoured the body of the young Hondscio.

And when Grendel had finished his horrid meal, the beast straightened a little his vast form and looked now to the left, now to the right, until his gaze fell upon the length of Beowulf. Then the milk-white eyes burned with a dull light that was like the light of the moon, and slowly, slowly Grendel moved toward the dais.

But Beowulf, stung with loathing, leaped from his bed.

SILENTLY they fought in the fog-strewn hall of Heorot. Silently their bodies twisted and bent, this way and that, and Beowulf kept Grendel's huge hands with their long claws of sharp bone from him, and Grendel in turn sought to tear apart the quick body that slipped so easily through his arms and legs.

All about them lay the sleeping earls, and not one moved in the deep magic of his slumber as the two fought that silent fight.

Their bodies wove in and out among the sleepers, and Beowulf felt the hot reek of Grendel's breath upon his cheek, and the sweat stood out on Beowulf's broad brow and ran down into his eyes and blinded him. And Grendel's huge hands sought over and over again to clasp his opponent's head, to crush it in their iron grip.

Then the fight became a deadly struggle in one far corner of the hall, and neither one gained any advantage over the other. Then Beowulf slipped. On the earthen floor of Heorot they fell together and the force of

their fall made the earth tremble, as when two giants fight in mortal combat.

Beowulf

But Grendel's hold lessened, and fear smote the heart of the fiend. He strove only to free himself from Beowulf's grasp and flee into the night, away from this white youth whose strength was the strength of thirty men.

And now Beowulf had the upper hand, and flew at the giant's throat. But here his hands clutched at thick scales upon which he could get no grip. Grendel nearly took the advantage, but before he could seize Beowulf, the lord of Geatsland had fastened both mighty hands upon the monster's arm, and with a sudden twist that forced a groan of agony from Grendel's lips, leaped behind him, forcing the imprisoned arm high up Grendel's back, and the beast fell prone on the floor.

Now came the final struggle, and sweat poured from Beowulf, while from Grendel there oozed a slimy sap that smelled like vinegar, and sickened Beowulf. But he clung to the monster's arm, and slowly, slowly he felt its great muscles and sinews give way, and as his foot found Grendel's neck, he prayed to all the gods for help, and called upon his father Ecgtheow for strength to sustain him in this desperate effort.

And the mighty arm of Grendel gave way in the terrible hands of Beowulf, and, with a piercing shriek that shook the gilded rafters of Heorot, Grendel stumbled forward, leaving in Beowulf's hands the gory arm.

At that very moment the spell that lay upon the sleeping warriors of Geatsland was broken, and the thirteen remaining earls struggled, as Beowulf had lately struggled, with the nightmare that was in their eyes, and swam out of sleep into waking.

Beowulf fell back upon the dais, the bleeding arm of Grendel in his hands. And Grendel, with a prolonged and ghastly wail, his blunt fangs gnashing together in dumb fury, stumbled toward the door, and before

Beowulf could recover, the fiend was away into the fog which swallowed him as surely and completely as though he had plunged into the everlasting sea.

And Beowulf, his magic-dazed companions crowding and babbling behind him in the doorway of Heorot, looked out into the fog-wet night, and the only sound that came to their dulled ears was the steady drip, drip, drip of the mist from the black trees.

WHEN dawn crept clear and untroubled across the woodland and touched the gold-bright hall of Heorot, there came from all quarters the subjects and servants of Hrothgar the king. In twos and threes they came at first, then in a great crowd, for the sleep of the world had been troubled the previous night, and now, half eager, half in consuming fear, the lords and peasantry of Daneland hurried to great Heorot.

At the wide doorway they rushed, and then, in amaze and wonder, they stopped: for within the hall there was a sight which for a moment made them afraid to enter, and those in front were held spellbound by what they saw, and those behind pushed eagerly forward in order to see.

For high toward the roof-tree of Heorot the brawny men of Geatsland were hoisting the mangled arm and torn shoulder of Grendel, and the people marveled at the sight of this arm, the largest and most terrible arm in all the world, the torn sinews hanging dead, the red ooze of the beast's blood clotted and caked on the cruel curved fingers with their hooked talons of bone.

Upon the dais of the king stood Beowulf, wrapped close in his scarlet mantle, his yellow hair about his head like a golden cloud, and his sea-blue eyes flashing with the pride of a conqueror.

Then the crowding people flocked into the hall, and a shout went up from a hundred throats as the arm swung high from the roof. And men hastened away to the bower of Hrothgar, and summoned the king and his lady Wealhtheow to view this token of the stricken Grendel.

And the king and queen entered Heorot speedily, and hastened to Beowulf. They grasped his two hands in theirs, and Hrothgar spoke in a loud voice, praising him:

"Beowulf, son of strong Ecgtheow, hail! This is truly an end to Grendel. Thrice blessed are you, my son, and upon you may all the rewards of the gods be showered. You have delivered Daneland from a curse that has been the undoing of our people and of our power during twelve long years. Again and yet again, hail to you, Beowulf, great hero of Geatsland!"

Then the lady Wealhtheow the Beautiful praised him also, and hung upon his arm, and called her servants to prepare a great feast for all the people. And the feasting and drinking lasted all that day and well into the night.

UT the day following, there suddenly arrived before Hrothgar a messenger, his face all twisted with fear, and his legs so shaking beneath him that they could scarce support his frame. And so distraught was this wild-eyed man that Hrothgar and Wealhtheow and Beowulf and all those who were then in Heorot clustered about him.

"Speak!" cried the queen, whose face was pale. "What new horror have you come to relate? For you have fear written black in your eyes. Speak!"

Turning to Hrothgar, the messenger fell upon his knees and lifted a stricken face to his master:

"My lord, I bring terrible news to you. I have just come from the great hall, where I have beheld a most grievous sight. My lord Aescher, the Good and Wise, lies dead upon the threshold of Heorot, most foully murdered by some new fiend, his head severed from his body, his limbs crushed to nought. Haste you, my lord, for this is the greatest of all disasters."

Forthwith Hrothgar and his queen hastened to Heorot and there too came Beowulf and his earls, not knowing of the new misfortune. And once again they found the vast hall a scene of death and destruction. Grendel's arm was missing from the roof-tree and the body of Aescher lay mangled before their horrified gaze.

Then Hrothgar turned away and folding his mantle about his head, wept silently, for Aescher was the most cherished of all his earls, the wisest of counselors, the dearest of friends.

Wealhtheow turned to the wide-eyed Beowulf.

"This," cried she, "is the work of dead Grendel's monster-mother, avenging her monster-son. O Beowulf, your work is not yet done. We had forgot this other curse in our too-soon happiness. Will you seek out this fiend and slay her as you have slain her dreaded offspring? Already you have rid us of Grendel, and now we look to you to save us from his mother's vengeance. I fear unending desolation for all of us unless she, too, is destroyed."

At these words Beowulf cast his scarlet cloak from his broad shoulders and seized his sword. He called to his valiant earls:

"Come, men! Let us seek this new monster before the world darkens again into night."

Then to the shaken king he said, "O Hrothgar, I pray that you will let horses be brought to carry us, for we must hasten to track the foul thing to her lair ere the scent is cold on the ground."

At this, Black Unferth, son of Ecglaf, stepped forth from among the crowding earls, and in his hands was the mighty shaft of his black sword, called Hrunting.

"Beowulf, son of Ecgtheow," he cried, "you came amongst us a stranger, and I am filled with shame in that I doubted you. Take my good sword Hrunting, my magic sword, for it will aid you in this new adventure that comes to try your strength, a strength that comes, surely, from the gods themselves. Let us bury our past differences and be friends, and I will follow you to the very edge of the world."

Then Beowulf embraced Unferth like a brother, and holding aloft the dark Hrunting, and with Hrothgar upon one hand and Wealhtheow upon the other hand he passed out through the great door of Heorot. Down the flight of long shallow steps they walked, and mounted at once the fine swift horses that awaited them below in the streaming sunshine.

SWIFTLY, swiftly they rode, Beowulf upon a great white charger and the king beside him on a horse as black as midnight. Their trappings and harness glinted with gold and silver and precious *Beowulf* jewels, and behind them rode the Danish lords and the earls of Geatsland, their armor gleaming in the sun as they rode after their leaders.

Huge dogs flung their enormous bodies along the way, having quickly picked up the powerful scent of Grendel and his monster-mother.

On and on they rode, but the sun at last was clouded over and the heavens lowered upon them, while distant thunder sounded and forked lightning streaked blue the inclosing gloom.

All day they rode, nor did they once pause to refresh their horses or themselves.

On and on, over moor and fenland, through wide valleys they rode, until finally they came to a mere, deep hidden in an encircling wood of tangled burnt-out trees. The lake was small, but strange and evil vapors rose from its surface and the water moved as though things of monstrous shape and size swam just below the water, waiting for whatever prey might fall to them.

Above the mere two great vultures with blood-red wings hovered in the foul-rising vapors, crying hungrily to each other, circling and circling.

The tracks of the monsters stopped short at the water's edge and the great dogs ran round and round the mere, but there was no further scent, and, sitting down upon their haunches, the hounds mournfully gave tongue.

The darkness thickened, and while the lords and their retainers lined the shores of the lake, looking for they knew not what, Beowulf threw off his scarlet cloak and was buckling the black sword Hrunting to his belt.

"I go into the mere," he cried, "after this monster-woman."

A murmur of horror went up from those assembled on the strand.

"Yes, but I go alone," he warned, as several stepped to his side, cast- ing off their cloaks. "I go alone. Wait here upon the shore for me. I will return, but when, I know not."

Then he fell on one knee before Hrothgar in homage, and embraced each of his followers. They crowded round him, protesting at his folly, but Beowulf was firm in his resolve and bade them wait upon his returning.

Fully armed, he ran swiftly into the lake, a shout on his lips, his fair hair streaming like light, and the leaden waters closed thickly over him, and the lake shuddered on all its surface, and Beowulf disappeared from sight.

OWN, down, down he sank. At first he could see nothing, and the dark water sang in his ears and lay about his body like a thick mantle. He felt things brushing against his legs and body, soft things that slipped and glided. At these he swung the sword Hrunting, but so noiseless and slimy were the invisible creatures at which he slashed that he could not tell whether his blows found their mark or not.

But gradually, as he sank, the darkness lessened, and he looked about him with wonder.

The water was now luminous, as if lighted by unseen fires of phosphorus and sulphur. Immense sea-animals and fish swayed past him in the mysterious light, and each, as he passed, threw at him an evil glance from its glowing eyes of red or green or sapphire blue. Their scales glinted like beaten gold, and his sword glanced from their sides as from fine armor.

Below him he saw fantastic forests of living coral, and many-colored sea-flowers, but (this was a strange thing) he never seemed to reach those deep sea-forests, for ever as he sank, the tops receded from him.

He was attacked by huge swarms of poisonous jelly-fish which sparkled in their strange whirlings. These he cut through valiantly, and tore their clinging masses from his limbs.

Once a hundred-armed monster caught him from behind, and he thought that he was lost. The snake-like tendrils coiled and twisted about his body, but he turned in a flash and sank Hrunting into the vile body until the long arms were loosened and the water was stained black from its blood.

Down, down, down he sank, through that shimmering and silent world, till he began to wonder when he would come upon what he sought so eagerly.

Again he looked below, and this time he saw in the far depths a ruddy

glow, as from, this time, a real fire of coals. He found himself sinking more rapidly now, and the water lay more lightly about him.

He looked up, trying to pierce the blue gloom through which he had come, but as he looked something seized him about the waist fiercely, and before he could recover from this new attack he found himself swiftly dragged into a glowing cave, brilliantly lighted from a great fire on a hearth, and clinging to his body the most loathsome hag he had ever beheld.

Her hair was a growth of long hissing snakes that twisted and writhed about her head. Her face was almost completely hidden by them, and all he could see was a hideous gaping mouth filled with sharp green fangs, and eyes that burned at him like live silver.

He was clutched by bony arms covered with thick rank hair, and the powerful lean body of the hag was clothed in strips of blackened fish-skins, foul-smelling and slimy.

She was of great height, Beowulf saw, but so bent was she that he looked down into her eyes, gleaming through the knotted coils of serpents. Her great jaws snapped at him and a horrid slime dripped from her purple lips.

All this Beowulf saw in a moment as he stood in her vicious grip, and while she devoured him with her eyes he had time to gage his position.

The fire in the waterless cave burned on an open hearth, and the place curved high above them as though within a giant bowl. The floor was covered with black sand, dry underfoot. And in a far corner Beowulf saw a massive shape which he knew to be Grendel.

The snakes of the monster-mother's hair hissed at him, her breath came hot and evil upon his face, and so slimy was her foul lean body that he could not hold her.

Her great claw-fingers sank into his flesh, his skin crept with the sickening touch of her, and they struggled there at the bottom of the world, in a cave under the water, and the great heart of Beowulf smothered him in his breast with a fear that was like nothing he had ever felt. Sweat poured from him, his legs melted under him like wax, there was a spell upon him that drained him of all strength.

He managed to draw his sword Hrunting, but so protected by magic was that mother of Grendel that try as he would Hrunting would not pierce her body and at last clattered to the floor from his numb hand. The fiend twisted this way and that, and with each twist the horrible hands reached nearer and nearer to his throat, and he grew weaker and weaker, and shorter and faster came his stifled breath.

He managed to lock his leg round one of the monster's, and then with all his fast-fleeing strength he seized the hag and threw her. But in falling she fell upon him, and now the loathsome, grinning jaws were close above his face, and the sharp claws found his throat.

But for a moment, the smallest moment in the world, she relaxed her hold, so sure was she of her prey, and in that little moment the magic was lifted, and Beowulf with a great cry hurled her from him.

· 58 ·

Once more on his feet, he staggered to the wall of the cave, and found, suddenly, in his grasp, the hilt of an old sword which was driven deep into the wall. But the fiend was on him again now with a strangled cry of terror. *Beowulf* Beowulf clutched the old sword with both hands, and with a great heave drew it from the wall, and so great was the force of the blow he struck Grendel's mother that he cut clean through her body.

Then all the spells dropped from him, and he stood panting above the dead monster. And he saw that the fire of the hearth had leaped high to the roof of the cave. Quickly Beowulf cut off Grendel's head where he lay in the corner of the cave, and then threw the two bodies to the flames.

Holding in one strong hand the head of Grendel, and in the other the magic sword he had found, Beowulf ran to the entrance of the cave and surged up through the black night of the water.

But on his way up he noticed that he was no longer attacked by the water-beasts and fish, while in his hand the blade of the magic sword, dissolved by the poison blood of Grendel's mother, melted away, until only the carven hilt remained in his grasp.

Up, up, up through the dark waters he floated, and all about him was a silence red from the blood of his victims.

ON THE shore of the lake into which Beowulf had plunged Hrothgar and his retainers had stayed for some time, but at last, giving up all hope of ever beholding the hero again, they returned to their homes. Only the thirteen Geatish earls remained, waiting for their lord. Some of these, it is true, wished to go back, saying that their leader had drowned in the lake, or that some demon had destroyed him. But these sad doubts were not held by all, and they finally agreed to remain for the longest possible time, in accordance with their lord's request.

Then suddenly one of their number, who had been watching the surface of the lake more hopefully than the others, cried out:

"See, my comrades, the water is stained with blood! What can it be? Is this the blood of Beowulf or of some monster with whom he has fought?"

And as all the earls gathered at the lakeside, a great heaving of the reddened water now took place, and under the astonished gaze of those who watched, the waters parted and Beowulf rose to the surface with a tremendous shout of joy.

When he reached the shore, they clustered about him, eager to hear what had happened. But he would tell them nothing, save that he had slain the monster-mother, and he showed them the hilt of the magic sword and the gory head of Grendel. The rest of the story, he told them, they would hear in Hrothgar's presence, and he urged them to make ready and post quickly thither with their glad news.

They mounted their horses, and singing the songs of conquerors, they rode toward the hall of Heorot.

There was great rejoicing when at last they arrived at the great hall, and a banquet was prepared, such a banquet as had never before been seen in all the land of the Danes or throughout the North.

The feasting and drinking went on far into the night, and many were the speeches made praising the courage and strength of Beowulf. And loudest of all praise came from the lips of Black Unferth, and all the earls marveled at his shining words.

Dawn broke upon the vast company, and at last Beowulf declared that now his mission in the land of the Danes was over, and that he and his earls must take their departure for their own shore.

Then Hrothgar the king rose in his place and said:

"Beowulf, my adopted son, you have accomplished great things for me and my countrymen. We thank the gods for your sending, and we wish to make some return to you and your earls for your valorous deeds."

And he commanded his servants and they came forward bearing rich presents of armor and harness for horses. There were goodly swords for the lords of Geatsland, and coffers of gold and silver and rare jewels, more than each man could carry on his own back, for himself.

There were carven drinking-horns for the King of Geatsland and fleecy woolens for Hygd the queen, stout shields of hide, bound with precious metal, helmets of beautiful workmanship and plumed with great wings, belts studded with gems, and many other gifts of surpassing value.

Later that morning Beowulf, together with his earls, and all the great treasure that Hrothgar had bestowed on him, set sail.

A vast multitude collected upon the shore of the sea to see the noble earls embark, and among them was none happier than that ancient Guardian of the Beach who had watched over their boat in their absence.

As the sails filled with the fresh wind, the shouts from those upon the beach thundered out with immense good-will. Banners fluttered in the morning breeze, and Beowulf's ship was turned toward distant Geatsland.

And thus ended, in surpassing joy and thanksgiving, Beowulf's adventures among the Danes.

WHICH TELLS of how a DRAGON appeared in Geatsland, and how Beowulf and Wiglaf destroyed it, and how sleep came to Beowulf.

MANY years passed, during which we know very little of what befell our hero Beowulf. He returned safely to Geatsland after his adventures among the Danes, and he was received with great acclaim at the court of his uncle Hygelac, and was hailed as the greatest of all living heroes in the North. Minstrels roamed the land singing of his deeds of strength and valor.

At last, however, death came to Hygelac during a momentous battle with the Frisians and the Franks, those warlike tribes, and his son Heardred became king in Hygelac's place. But Heardred's reign was not long, and after him Beowulf came to the throne of Geatsland.

THEN there began a long and happy period in the country of the Geats. Prosperity rained upon them. The Geatish warriors were ever successful in battle, and the treasury was filled to bursting with gold and silver and precious stones and armor.

The nets of the fisher-folk were so laden with sea-spoils that they could scarce be lifted. The crops in the fields increased so that the people were well fed and contented even throughout the long and arduous winters.

Great contests were held at the hall of Beowulf at frequent intervals, and all the heroes from near and far gathered there to match the strength and skill of the Geatish warriors.

So passed the happy years, and Beowulf grew in stature and dignity and strength. A vast beard fell from his cheeks, and as he moved among his people many sought to touch the hand that had slain Grendel. For Beowulf's fame was known not only in his own land but across the wide seas, and his enemies (for he had excellent ones) trembled at the mention of his name and thought twice before they went to engage him in battle.

The years passed, but no adventure equal to the slaying of Grendel and that monster's mother came to test out Beowulf's valor and strength. And the king waxed restless for a great adventure, for his years were now many and he felt that a not long season remained to him on earth.

ONE night, when the winter was at its deepest, and the king sat in his mead-hall with all his lords about him, there came a knocking at the door. When the servants opened to the knocking, there entered the shabbiest visitor that had ever crossed that noble threshold.

The servants would have thrown the stranger out again, so disgraceful was his attire, had not Wiglaf, son of Weohstan, called to them to let the visitor remain, for there was something in the man's face that caught the earl's interest.

"Who are you?" demanded Wiglaf. "Whence come you? Speak, and do not fear, for no one will harm you. I see your knees shaking with fright and cold, and your eyes are wild with want of sleep and strange things that you have seen. Come and eat, my good man, and then you shall tell your story to the king."

But the stranger made a sign with his head that Wiglaf took for a denial, and so led him, a little roughly, before Beowulf.

"This fellow," the noble Wiglaf said, "will not say his name or whence he comes. But to you, my dear lord, he will speak, I know."

Then Beowulf bent on him his kindly-strong gaze and bade the visitor have no fear. The man fell on his knees before the king and spoke in a high voice:

"Great king, I have no name and am but a poor escaped slave from a Frankish galley, and I am seeking my own home in the Northland. Early this morning, faint from cold and hunger and want of rest, I came upon a deep barrow in which I discovered, sleeping, the hugest dragon, surely, in all the wide world. At first I was so overcome with fear that I fled from the place. But after a while, when I got back my breath, I was taken with a burning curiosity, and when my hair had lain down again upon my head, I returned, and there I saw, heaped round and about the sleeping dragon, the lordliest treasure that ever man beheld in one place together. Gold and jewels—" the slave raised his arms high and wide—"so much that twenty cart-loads would make no diminishment that the eye could see."

Beowulf leaned forward in his great chair, his vast hands gripping the carven arms.

"Slave," he cried in a loud voice, "if you lie, I will have you first beaten like a dog and then torn limb from limb until you are dead!"

But the stranger did not flinch under the blue fire of the king's glance. Instead, he drew from beneath his tattered cloak a wondrous jeweled cup, set about with a hundred brilliants of all the rainbow's colors, and standing upon a base of purest gold, most delicately carved.

"Lord," he replied simply, "I do not lie."

The court crowded about, better to see this marvel of workmanship and worth. Beowulf handled it lovingly, and held it to the firelight.

But at this point the escaped slave was seen to totter in a faint and quickly he was led away to be given food and warm clothes and a bench to lie upon.

Then Beowulf the king stood up in his place and said to the assembled company:

"My friends, you have heard this man's tale, and you see that he is no idle spinner of yarns who would obtain food and shelter on a bitter winter's night, for he has shown us this wondrous cup of gold and jewels. Surely there is no fairer goblet on earth, and this slave says that whence this came there is more and still more treasure. My comrades, eleven men I want, who will follow me to the foul dragon's lair. This grave menace must be destroyed before he wakens and finds that he has been discovered and plundered. Eleven of you, then, to my side. There will be deeds of bravery for all, and of treasure more than each man can dream."

Then Wiglaf, the son of Weohstan, the best beloved of Beowulf's earls, stepped forward, but as he opened his lips to swear allegiance to his king, the night was shattered by a roar that shook the roof of the hall and made the earth tremble underfoot.

The warriors, having laid aside their armor and swords, rushed to secure the door, but as confusion spread among them and women screamed, the roar persisted in its clangor and at the entrance door blue flames began to lick along the sill.

Then Beowulf cried in a loud voice to the court that they must escape from the monster until they could assume their weapons and armor, and secure the women against the hot anger of the furious dragon. So, in orderly manner, the company followed their king through a back way, leaving the vast hall in emptiness, the benches overturned, the fire on the hearths burning low.

DAWN came slowly over the snows lying heavy about the house of Wiglaf, and the wife of Beowulf's favorite earl was ordering her servants in their early tasks when Wiglaf burst in upon the family hearth. His face was drawn with rage and fear, and he embraced his wife with such impetuousness that the good lady became instantly consumed with the darkest of thoughts and forebodings.

"My lord," she cried, "what dread errand brings you hither at this hour from the king? Speak! Some disaster has befallen the world, that you should look so distraught."

And she hastened to relieve him of his great cloak.

But he put her away from him, and cried out in anguish:

"Dear lady, gather together all that we have of value which the servants can carry upon swift horses, for this night a dragon, the vastest dragon in all the world, has come upon our Geatsland, and even as I speak pursues his hideous way across the snow toward this our home. Already the mead-hall of the king is naught but a heap of smoldering ashes, and the granaries and storehouses of our people are hiding the sun from the world with the smoke of their burning. Make haste, I pray you, my lady, and fetch me the biggest of my swords and the stoutest of my armor. Then get you gone to the caves by the Whale's Headland while we pursue this hellish demon to his lair.

"I go at once to my king. There is such death and destruction abroad this morn as never man has beheld, and the ruins of our fairest farms and halls are dotting the white land with sorrow and woeful suffering."

Then Wiglaf's wife brought him his great broadsword and his

stoutest armor, and embraced him tenderly ere he strode to the door.

Even now the sky was brown with dense smoke, and a vast and sinister rumbling was heard upon the air, proclaiming the steady and awful approach of the dragon.

Gathered together in the depths of the great forest, Beowulf and his band of eleven trusted warriors held a council of war.

There arose a warm debate concerning how the dragon should be fought. Some thought they should attempt to slay him while he wrought destruction. Others, again, would lure him, if possible, to a high cliff, and force him into the boiling sea below. Yet others were in favor of letting him wreak his vengeance at will upon the country-side until such time should come when, sated in his lust for killing, he might fall into an exhausted sleep and become fair game for their sharp swords.

Then Beowulf spoke:

"My lords, each of these three plans has excellent reasons for pursuing it. But it is my opinion that none of them is sufficient for our dear purpose.

"For, in the first instance, if we attack the dragon while he is yet roaring through the land, the creature will be able to retreat in any direction.

"In the second instance, it is not likely that he will permit himself to be forced over a cliff into the sea, for by all tokens he is a wily dragon and the treasure is close to his heart.

"And in the third instance, we cannot permit him to continue his depredations throughout the country-side, and further impoverish our people.

"Therefore, hear you what I have to say: It is necessary that we track this vile enemy to his very lair, there to slay him. For when he finds that Beowulf and his noble earls are gone to his barrow, then will he leave our halls and farms and seek to defend his heart's treasure. Let us away forthwith, for soon enough will he discover our ruse."

And Beowulf was right, for, even as he spoke, the dragon, writhing his way from the desolation or the king s country, was informed, by magic, of the plans that were being made for his destruction, and switching his scaly tail so that twenty stout trees fell at its movement, and snapping gigantic jaws in horrid rage, the creature hastened to protect that which he had guarded during three hundred years of sleepless vigilance.

NIGHT was coming down when at last Beowulf and his eleven earls approached the dragon's barrow. It lay deep in a dark and gloomy forest, and the only light was the reflection of the dead day upon the ground-snow. The tall trees stood naked in their places, and

all about hung a cold stillness which was broken only by the trampling of the adventurers upon the crunching snow.

It was quite dark now, as they neared the spot, and through the dim night they beheld in the distance a reddish glow. Nearer they came, until, peering through the dense wood, they saw a broad clear space among the trees.

At one side was an old burial-mound, and at its entrance there issued in hissing gusts the red steam of the dragon's hot breathing. All about the place, the snow was trampled by huge feet and the tree trunks were blackened and scorched.

Then brave Beowulf drew his earls about him and said to them:

"I go alone to engage this dragon. You shall remain here at the clearing's edge in readiness to stand by me in case I fail. For I am an old man now, and it comes to me, as in a dream, that this will be my last adventure, my final fight."

Then gripping his vast shield of iron surely in his left hand, and in his right the noble sword Naegling, Beowulf advanced to meet the dragon.

But his earls, all those trusted earls, save only that faithful and loving lord Wiglaf, were seized with a sudden fear, and fled away into the darkness of the night and the shelter of the encircling forests. King Beowulf did not see their fleeing, as his eyes were upon the mouth of the barrow, and his ears were dimmed by the noise of the dragon's breathing and the swish-swish of the angry body within the cave's fastness.

Then Beowulf cried out in a ringing voice:

"Come out, O most foul fiend, for Beowulf, King of Geatsland, Prince of Weders, and son of great Ecgtheow, stands without and calls you to battle. Come out, I say, arch-dragon, and pit your vaunted strength against my strength, which is the greatest known in all this cold Northland!"

And Wiglaf, standing ready and alone at the circle's edge, laughed a clarion challenge to the dragon's undoing.

For a moment there was a death-like stillness in the night. No sound *Beowulf* came from the cave, and no steamy breath, and no dull glare of fire. Then with sudden roaring that caused the night to splinter and the earth to quiver in horrified response, the lordliest dragon in all the world rushed from its lair.

Over ten ells in length it measured, from the proud head to the poisoned tail-tip, and its vast body was covered with scales of brass as big as plates and thicker, each, than three fingers. Its forefeet were armed with six-inch claws of razor edge, and helped support a head so large and terrible that Beowulf marveled for a moment at the size. Its eyes were of green fire, its wide nostrils belched red flame and steam, and the immense jaws dripped livid ooze as they snapped in hideous savagery. So great was the issuing heat that Beowulf held up his shield, else he would have perished upon the spot.

Again came a moment's pause while the two antagonists stood firm and eyed each other, each gaging his own strength and that of his adversary.

Battle came upon them with the swiftness of lightning. The still forest was filled with the clamor of their combat. Beowulf slashed out bravely, but his good sword Naegling glanced helplessly against the brazen scales of the dragon's armor, and so great was the heat of the creature's breath that Beowulf was forced to resort to cunning in an attempt both to wear out his enemy and keep himself from being burned to death.

He wove this way and that, feinting now here, now there, until the dragon was so bewildered with this wonderful display of agility that his roaring grew louder and more terrible, and the violent swing of his huge body grew wider and wilder. Trees fell to earth at the flick of his tail, the snow melted beneath his breath, and his green eyes bit through the steam-clouds of his breathing.

And always Beowulf fought for the advantage of a well-placed thrust of his sword, for he knew that every dragon has its vulnerable spot, and this he sought to find.

Back and forth over the hard ground they raged. Now the dragon seemed the victor and Beowulf spent and weakening—but only to renew his attack.

And time stood still in the black night, and the stars in their courses stayed to watch this struggle of giants.

Beowulf's breath came short and stifled, his arms grew weak from the weight of his great sword and shield, and this last grew so hot that it no longer served to protect him from the living furnace which he fought. His strong legs shook beneath him, and short cries were wrung from his throat. The encircling trees swam before his faltering eyes, the heavens seemed to close down upon him.

Then at last to his aid came Wiglaf the faithful, and Beowulf's ears were gladdened by the sound of his dear friend's shout, and new strength streamed through his veins. Together they fought, side by side, and the dragon gave way to their onslaught.

But in one wide sweep of the dragon's tail Beowulf was caught, and he sank to the ground broken, at last, in body. But Wiglaf, fresh in the fray, with a great cry of rage, found the weak spot in the dragon's armor, and into the heart of the beast sank his good sword to the hilt.

No sound came from the dragon. But he rose to his full and terrible height in great majesty of dying, and fell prone beside Beowulf.

Then there went up a shout from the cowardly earls who had hidden in the forest to watch the fight in safety, and they crowded about their dying king. But Wiglaf drove them away, saying:

"Away, wretches of faithlessness! Not for you the honors of a battle you feared to engage in. Away, cowards! Our king is done to death in a noble adventure, to save you and your foul breed from the dragon's wrath."

Then turning to Beowulf, he knelt at his side, took him dying into his arms, and loosened the helmet from his brow.

"O my dear master," he cried over him, "leave us not in your hour of triumph!"

"Nay," answered Beowulf, " 'tis not my triumph but that of a faithful friend, my Wiglaf. Take the treasure, do what you will with it. But . . . but let me have one piece of it about me as I die. For I die soon, my friend . . . so haste you . . . haste . . ."

Then Wiglaf went into the dragon's barrow and beheld there the greatest treasure, surely, in all the wide world. And he selected from the heaped-up gold and jewels a wondrous crown of glittering gems, and this he placed upon the brow of his king.

"I die," whispered Beowulf, "and I forgive those others—those foolish ones who deserted me in my hour. Farewell, good Wiglaf, my own true friend. Make a barrow for me upon the Whale's Headland. Farewell . . . and now I shall sleep . . . the longest sleep."

Beowulf

And so died Beowulf, greatest and truest of all the early heroes of legend.

HEY carried his body to the Whale's Headland, where a great barrow was made for him, and Wiglaf ordered all the treasure of the dragon's cave to be brought, that it should burn most rightly upon the funeral pyre of Beowulf the king. And so great was their sense

· 79 ·

of the fitness of this, and their sorrow at loss of their excellent lord, that not one of the cowardly earls lifted his voice in protest against Wiglaf's order.

From far and near the men and women of Geatsland gathered to honor and mourn their dead lord and marvel at the great bulk of the dragon.

And beside the huge barrow upon the Whale's Headland, above the darkling sea, many hands raised a vast funeral pyre of scented logs and evergreen boughs.

Then the dragon was dragged to the precipice, and when it fell into the gray sea far, far below, a loud shout went up from a hundred throats as it slipped to the lonely waves.

They brought Beowulf's body to the pyre. He was borne upon his mighty shield, the great sword Naegling was laid upon his breast, and the jeweled crown from the cave was on his brow, and he was carried upon the shoulders of six earls.

Behind the bier walked fifty barons of Geatsland, the highest and mightiest in all the North; and following them, fifty musicians, with horns and pipes, making a doleful music.

Three times the sad procession marched around the high pyre, and the music rang out clear and loud, and the weeping multitude fell upon its knees.

Darkness came down upon the land, and the sound of the waves beneath the Whale's Headland grew more and more insistent, as though the sea, remembering Beowulf's early mastery of it, lamented also his passing.

Now, at the last, Beowulf was laid upon the sweet-scented pyre, and all about him were heaped the countless treasures from the dragon's mound. Then Wiglaf approached with two flaming torches, to do the dead king honor. Proclaiming the greatness of his dear lord, he held high above his head the flares and plunged them into the pyre. The flames leaped up, staining crimson the dark night, and so great was the glare from the burning that the stars put out their light, and the sea stopped its sad mourning.

Higher and higher rose the flames and with them the lamentations of

Beowulf the people. And the noble earls took up again their sad marching about the burning pyre, and all night long they marched, until at long last there was nothing left of the pyre but a high mound of gray ashes in the gray dawn.

THUS passed to his own gods Beowulf, King of Geatsland, in the North.